The Grumpalump

Written by
Sarah Hayes

Illustrated by
Barbara Firth

Clarion Books
New York

The bear stared at the grumpalump.
The lump grumped.

For David
with love
S.H.

Clarion Books
a Houghton Mifflin Company imprint
215 Park Avenue South, New York, NY 10003

Text copyright © 1990 by Sarah Hayes
Illustrations copyright © 1990 by Barbara Firth

First published in Great Britain by
Walker Books Ltd., London.

Printed in Hong Kong.

Library of Congress Cataloging-in-Publication Data
Hayes, Sarah
The grumpalump / by Sarah Hayes: illustrated by Barbara Firth.
p.   cm.
Summary: All the animals try to get a reaction out of the mysterious
lumpy grumpalump, but nothing happens until the gnu blows into it and gets an inflated surprise.
ISBN 0-89919-871-6   PA ISBN 0-618-04033-1
[1. Animals—Fiction. 2. Hot air balloons—Fiction]
I. Firth, Barbara, ill.   II. Title
PZ7.H314873Gr   1991   90-33335
[E]—dc20   CIP
                             AC

10 9 8 7 6 5 4 3 2

The bear stared and
the cat sat on the grumpalump.
The lump grumped.

The bear stared, the cat sat and
the mole rolled on the grumpalump.
The lump grumped.

The bear stared, the cat sat, the mole rolled and the dove shoved the grumpalump. The lump still grumped.

The bear stared, the cat sat,
the mole rolled, the dove shoved and
the bull pulled the grumpalump.
The lump still grumped.

The bear stared, the cat sat, the mole rolled, the dove shoved, the bull pulled and the yak whacked the grumpalump. The lump still grumped.

The bear stared, the cat sat, the mole rolled,
the dove shoved, the bull pulled,
the yak whacked and
the armadillo used it for a pillow.
But the lump still grumped.

Then
the
gnu
blew.

The lump grew plump, and got humps and
bumps, bits and bobs and
interesting knobs, and wings and
things attached with strings.
And still the gnu blew.

Then, to everyone's surprise,
the grumpalump began to rise.

The gnu drew breath
and clambered in.
The grumpalump began to grin.
"I'm off on a trip in my hot airship,"
said the gnu, and flew.
Absolutely true.

And how the bear stared.